The Unyielding of Monotony

By: Chinira Rhayne

© 2023

This is a literary work of fictious names, characters, places, incidents and situations. This literary expression is the result of the author challenging her imagination and being creative.

Any resemblance, actual person, locations, names either living or dead, business, companies, events are entirely a coincidence.

"Monotony is the law of nature. Look at the monotonous way the sun rises. The monotony of necessary occupation is exhilarating and life giving."

— <u>Mahatma Gandhi</u>

Introduction

The deepest threat to a meaningful life isn't a crisis; it is the slow quiet tyranny of the familiar circumstance. It's the insidious realization that you are living a perfectly manage, perfectly acceptable life-a life you can predict right down to the color of a tie you will wear on a random Tuesday.

You have a routine. You are successful. You pay your bills on time, yet when you look at the calendar, every week it blurs into the next, defined by the same meetings, the same errands and the same predictable outcomes. You feel the pull of life that is efficient but utterly devoid of surprise. Bad companies can influence good character. Not knowing oneself or avoiding authenticity can lead to a monotonous life, with suppression often used as a defense mechanism. Routine becomes comfortable, boredom feels good causing a person to avoid change because of the pain that can go with anything different. Over time, the pressures of careers, making money, the feeling of success and social status may disconnect you from your values, what's important in life and leave you feeling lost. Eventually, you realize that what you once prioritized might undermine your overall well-being, but awareness and action can still lead to transformations.

Pain is real.

Life is short.

Reality is sometimes fake.

Truth can vary.

Stories can differ.

Goals are attainable.

Boldness requires courage.

Chapter 1

The ducks were in their usual formation on the pond this morning. It was 7:35 AM and the light hit the kitchen counter at the same angle as it always does. As I prepared my usual breakfast, buttered toast, scrambled eggs and orange juice on the surface, I had achieved the dream. My home is large. It's squeezed with five bedrooms in the pool. My husband's lifestyle. Carter and I have a fulfilling life built on stability and predictability. I live by the old wisdom. If it's not broken, don't bother fixing it. That's wisdom. I realized it was a lie. What if the life you built isn't broken, but merely dormant? What if the relentless pursuit of stability is, in fact, the greatest threat to a meaningful existence? I had to create a routine so flawlessly efficient that it had successfully exiled surprise challenge and genuine aliveness.

We aim to achieve the American dream with financial security and plans for kids, pets, travel, and a relaxing retirement. I believe in doing things right the first time which will lead to a meaningful productive life.

After college, I became Silver Tree Architecture Concepts' first female Senior

Project Manager in Scottsdale, Arizona. Two years later, while competing against a rival firm for a major contract, I met Sylvester Carter—a consultant at that company, known for aggressive tactics and bulldog behavior. Despite warnings, I was determined to succeed in the business and gain as much money as I could. Not only did my firm win the contract, but I also met my future husband.

We spent so much of our time together, despite some coworkers' disapproval due to Sylvester's ethnicity. I value him for his character and abilities, not his background or culture. Our relationship was rooted in respect, affection, and dedication both personally and professionally. We supported each other in every way possible. We both made money. Lots of money!

We never competed against each other just thriving for long term success as a power couple.

Sylvester was adopted at age two by a Black family after the death of his biological parents. They died in a tragic car accident. With his parent being immigrants of Korea, he had no other relatives in America. His adoptive parents changed his name for pronunciation purposes, and he grew up with four older siblings in Phoenix, Arizona. Upon completing college, Sylvester decided to stay in Phoenix. As the youngest child, he received considerable attention from his family. He was spoiled rotten. Nothing about this man resemble Korea descent. The man had the swag of Justin Timberlake or Robin Thicke all in a sexy 6'0 nice physique package. His upbringing included education about both his own Korean and African American culture, with an emphasis on respect, discipline, dedication, and hard work. Sylvester is described as well-rounded, ambitious, very intelligent asset to society. Me on the other hand had a 360-degree upbringing. We came from two totally different spectrums of the world. But we found each other and fell in love. Me on the other hand had more drama than a little bit.

I was born Leroya Ashley Montgomery in Richmond, California, but was raised in Lynwood. My mom, Monika Webster, pursued an engineering degree from University of California (UCLA) while supporting our family working at Popeyes after my father received a 25-year prison sentence. Before my dad was sentenced to prison time, we didn't want for anything. No matter what my dad had to do, we had our needs and some. My dad was a professional street pharmacist. He ran to an entire side of Lynwood. He had people working for him like Frank Lucas of American Gangster. During my childhood, I took on responsibilities for my two younger brothers, Leroy Jr. and Dayshawn to help my mom. By age 6, I was changing diapers; by age 8, I was preparing meals; and by age 11, I regularly managed tasks such as getting all of us ready for school in the mornings for school. I packed Dayshawn's baby bags for daycare at night for efficiency, ironed clothes for Leroy Jr. and myself, and set them out each evening after our baths. Mom wanted to keep our lifestyle together, so she stopped working at Popeyes and started being a stripper at the Donkey Butt Poney Strip Club. All the ballers were known to visit this club. Mom would come home with garbage bags full of money. I would help her separate the bills. Most nights she made between $2000 to $3000. The men were crazy about my mom. She was very pretty; slim body frame and most men said her butt was too big for her to carry around.

After Mom finally crashed from another late night, I was the one left to manage the morning. I walked a Shawn to Miss Kitty's daycare, knowing the interrogation was coming. Miss Kitty always pushed. Why wasn't my mother here? I had a different flimsy explanation for every day of the week, designed to deflect her nosiness and protect. A family secret. I promised my father I would look after my siblings, and I wouldn't let him down. My solo caretaking was a fragile thing, and I knew that too many questions would bring the whole arrangement crashing down.

But one morning, Miss Kitty skipped the usual questions and went straight for the attacks. "It's an adult job to bring their children inside," she told my mom, who had, for once, actually made the trip!

Mom did not flinch. "You should learn to mind your own business and attend to your personal responsibility." She fired back. The retort was so sharp, so perfect, that the entire staff burst out laughing and Miss Kitty Space. I watched, stunned, as if it on her face went from smug to purple. The incident was a brief, satisfying victory, but it also made things more dangerous. Now that she has been publicly ashamed, Miss Kitty would be only looking harder for reasons to cause us trouble.

Leroy Jr. and I attended English Creek Academic Institution; he enrolled in kindergarten while I was in fifth grade. It was a private school. Mom made sure the tuition was paid faithfully. I know my dad left her money to help hold us down for a while. I saw a duffle bag full of hundred-dollar bills in the back of her closet. I took responsibility for the wellbeing of my younger brothers and would intervene when necessary to protect my mom at all costs. My academic record proved consistent achievement, as I kept straight A's and avoided disciplinary incidents, yet remained assertive in the face of bullying. I did not play when it came down to protecting my little brothers and myself. I developed strategies to refrain from unnecessary attention from school officials. I did everything I could to protect my mom from getting visit from social services. School personnel tended to be nosey, yet observant, often making assumptions about students' home environments. We were able to navigate these interactions effectively. I made sure we attended school every day. No one knew I was 11 years old raising two younger siblings. Occasionally, I had to falsify my mom's signature on our homework if she had not signed it upon her return from the night club. My mom ensured we were equipped with up-to-date fashion, new sneakers, clothing, backpacks, and school supplies. She often sent snacks to the other students just to throw a diversion. Our nutritional needs were met through a monthly food assistance benefit of $956. Furthermost, I did majority of the grocery shopping since I was preparing all the meals. I would fix mom a plate, leave it in the microwave for her.

By the time I reached high school, we moved to the New Wilmington Arms housing projects in Compton. I hated we had to trade our luxury home for a government subsidized rundown apartment. The area experienced various criminal activities such as drug dealing, violent incidents, and fights; activity occurred on a daily basis. Mom met a new guy that pulled her out of the club. He promised to provide a better lifestyle;

however, I beg for the difference. My mom received housing assistance and began working at a local hospital as a nurse assistant. Our stay there was intended to be temporary until my junior year, while my mom saved money to move us back to Lynwood. Leroy Jr, who was then in middle school, started associating with a well-known local gang for protection. His behavior changed—he skipped school, sold drugs, got into fights, and used marijuana. I hated this place. It smelled like old mildew, mothballs, and baby diapers. My mom, occupied with work and her personal life, did not notice these changes. Several different men lived with us over time. One of them, Lester Reynolds, was respected in the community due to his criminal record and street connections. He was my mom's new love bum. They were often on and off with their situationship. My mom used out food stamps to host gatherings that included Lester and his acquaintances. Her relationship with Lester led to changes in her behavior and social interactions within our home. Mom grew unfriendly, cold aloof and private. Her look changed. Her behavior changed. She stopped investing in herself, walked on eggs shells to appease Lester and stoke his childish narcissistic ego. He was in the bottom shelf grade compared to my dad. I never would have imagined my mom would have degraded herself to pick Lester. He reminded me of JJ Evans from Good Times with the mouth of a guppy fish with gold teeth. His breath always smelt like marijuana, alcohol, and rotten food.

During my father's incarceration at Pleasant Valley State Prison, I kept regular correspondence with him to keep him updated about developments concerning myself and our family. My father was acquainted with Lester from earlier interactions in the community and consistently expressed a strong dislike for him, rooted in their history about territory disputes within the projects and the city of Lynwood. My dad's reputation as a respected figure was notable—few dared to challenge him or his associates, including Lester. I believe that why he started dating my mom, to get back at my dad.

When my father's arrest occurred, reports surfaced that certain acquaintances had cooperated with law enforcement for lesser sentences, which introduced issues of trust within our street family. My father, Leroy Sr, typically remained well-informed about local hood community matters and the snitches. During this period, my mom experienced even more significant personal challenges; her first use of marijuana escalated to cocaine and frequent alcohol consumption, ultimately leading to daily drinking, snorting cocaine, and shooting up heroin. This progression coincided with Lester's frequent arrival from out of state trafficking kilos of drugs, although my mom did not perceive any connection to the direct drug business however it gave her unswerving asses to as much cocaine her body can consume. As a result of being stoned most days, she ceased discussing her aspirations to return to school or seek different employment. I slowly saw Lester ripping my mom apart from who is really is.

My anticipation for my father's release grew as he neared completion of his sentence, with parole possible in two years. Some say my dad was working with the feds as an informant for early release. I prayed he would come rescue my mom, myself and my brothers from a life of horror. I longed for stability and a sense of normalcy to return to our lives in Lynwood. My father, standing 6'4" and of mixed Hispanic and Black heritage, had a golden-brown complexion and dark curly hair. The ladies could not wait for my dad to touch down from prison. They often would ask me about him especially with them knowing my mom was Lesters girlfriend now. Throughout his imprisonment, I stayed intricately connected to him, unwavering in my belief in his innocence. My dad did nothing wrong with my eyes. All he was trying to do was provide for his family like everyone else in this world. Affectionately, he referred to me as his "little LAM," inspired by my name. I was sure to tell my dad everything that was going on in Lynwood. He always knew because he continued to have eyes and ears to the streets. He hated Lester, definitely the fact my mom being with him, strung out on drugs. I made it my business to see Dayshawn and Leroy Jr, stayed out the way of Lester and his entourage. We went to school, same as always but Leroy Jr begins looking up to Lester as father figure. My dad hated this with everything in his soul. He even sent words for Lester to leave my brother out of his street life, or dad would send heat (street trouble) after Lester. He mocked my dad's words, went harder in his actions, and gave my mom all the drugs she could handle. Some people in the neighborhood said mom was selling her body, organizing drug deals, and setting up people to be robbed by Lester and his crew. I saw signs of this ridiculousness every day. One day, I came home from school to find four men, dressed in black with hoodies, face mask and assault rifles on the kitchen table. Mom rushed us upstairs to avoid overhearing the criminal plan. I slowly tiptoed partially downstairs to hear the scheme. With the yelling and loud talking, I am sure the neighbors can hear the plan. I literally can't believe Lester has these idiots robbing someone. But then again, I can! Monika (my mom) was meeting another rival drug dealer at his trap house to have sex. While she is in action, Lester boys will swarm in, rob the trap house of drugs and money. Possibly killing anyone who gets in the way. I wanted to tell my dad, but by the time he got the letter, the hit would have been over.

Monika has lost her mind. I do not know whether the drugs are killing her brain cells or clouding her judgment of reality. I was afraid my mom would end up dead or serving time in prison with my dad. The thought of losing both parents did not sit well with me. Lester was a bum! There is no way, this man has any value to his morals or dignity to put a mother of three kids in danger to die over his stupid robbery plan.

Chapter 2

Fourth of July weekend; everyone was outside barbecuing, shooting craps, playing spades, and listening to loud music. Theres nothing like a project party until you have been here. There was no such thing as a party without a spade game, 40 oz's and loud talking. All the younger kids were running around playing football or tag. I would just look from my bedroom window; I did not like living there and I would rather stay in my room to read a book instead. The overwhelming smell of stank, marijuana, and alcohol from Lester and his friends became the normal aroma in the home. It was like lighting a bum scented Yankie Candle. I loved scented candles by Tina, myself. I would buy one for my room, every chance I could.

Our house felt like a trap house. My mom did not care what went on. I could not recognize her anymore. She was frail, butt sagging like a shitty baby diaper, eyes buck like a dear, and her hair was falling out. This was not the mom in knew from Lynwood. This mom lost her dreams of being an Engineer. I would look at her, and I swore some days, I saw a different person. Grandma Pearl, my dad's mom, would say, the devil has taken over! Her boyfriend, Lester had his crew, friends, clients, and tricks in our house every day. Some of the woman has been known to run licks and rob guys for him too. He was having sex with these women as well. I caught him with the woman my mom best friend. Ms. Charmaine was a whore! Any women that wore gold dental plates, drinks alcohol like a fish, smokes more than a hookah bar, had long dirty nasty fingernails, bootie shorts in the winter and thick acrylic toenails were nothing more than a skank seeking attention from anyone that will to entertain her. The only thing she had in common with my mom was Lester and free drugs.

That day, mom asked me to join her on the front porch to watch the local neighborhood girls as they practiced dance routines and take part in friendly competitions against each other. I saw their routines just about every day, which were like ones I had practiced before up in my bedroom, and occasionally imagined taking part in their activities.

It was not a good 15 minutes outside with her before we heard a loud commotion, screaming and yelling coming from a huge crowd towards the front of the apartment complex. A fight broke out! Yes, a fight! All I saw was several fists being thrown, bodies being slammed, titties hanging out bras, butt cheeks, nasty dirty draws showing and babies crying. Luckily, I did not see any wigs in the air, or shirts being completely ripped off. I yelled at my mom; *it is Dayshawn-* on the ground getting kicked by two older boys. We both ran over as fast as we could. I was in rage. I was a little ready to take my frustration out on anyone that wanted it. We pushed the boys off my brother, and I swung on the biggest one I could run up on. One of their boys' moms got upset and jumped on my mom, pulling her hair, slanging her to the ground. At that moment, the hood come out of me with every punch I was swinging to help my mom beat her ass. I must have had a blackout because the next thing I knew, Lester was scooping me up in his arms while dragging my mom and I back inside the house.

Although I had not previously been involved in a physical altercation, I seemed to have inherited my father's low tolerance for disrespect. Dayshawn sustained some serios injuries during the incident. I suggested that my mom take him to the hospital, but we did not have any health insurance. As an alternative, I provided him with a frozen pack of carrots from the freezer to reduce the swelling on his forehead. But I had no idea what to do about his bruise ribs and broken wrist.

My mom and Lester argued in her room about a fight she did not start—she was just defending Dayshawn, and I am trying to understand Lester's reasoning for yelling at my mom like she is a stray dog. Lester said unwanted attention will cause his business to suffer. Later things in their bedroom got quiet. I knew they were either having sex or snorting cocaine. They often did both. I shut my door, lay on my bed, and prayed to God to leave the projects. Incidents like this are common here, but it was the first time one of my brothers was involved. Dayshawn stayed with me that night, and Leroy Jr. did not return home. My mom became concerned only after school let her know about his frequent absences and tardiness. There were allegations that he took part in an incident at the Grove Manner complex resulting in another student's death; however, Leroy Jr denied any participation in the shooting. I believe he either saw the event or had information about those responsible, even if he was not directly involved. These rumors circulated throughout Compton, often worsened by individuals such as Ms. Charmaine. With her gossiping lips on someone else's life. She is always in someone else's business with her pissy smelling self. Part of me wanted to believe it was true because Lester always tried to tell Leroy Jr his fake gangster stories. Leroy Jr was selling drugs for Lester too. He is the man that put the first gun in Leroy Jr hand, taught him how to cook cocaine, bag it, and flip it. My dad would break out of prison if he knew this was happening. I wanted to tell him so badly, but I could not risk my dad getting into trouble and coping more time. My mom definitely did not care for as long as she could get high! All she wanted to do was smoke, snort or shoot up drugs. She was turning into a crack fem. (seriously addicted)

The unfortunate aspect of the situation was that Lester was aware my father would not condone Leroy Jr.'s involvement in illicit activities. My father and Lester ran in separate areas of the neighborhood, occasionally interacting and fighting while keeping mutual respect for each other's boundaries. My dad was also aware of my mom's crack dependent relationship with Lester and strongly disapproved of his influence on Leroy Jr., as he believed it placed Leroy Jr. at risk of future incarceration or even six feet under. He sent words several times through his friends to look out for Leroy Jr in the street game. My brother had a hot head like our dad. Always felt he had to live up to expectations of others or carry the legacy of my dad.

My mom declined to take us upstate to visit our father, ceasing all visits after beginning her relationship with Lester. Nevertheless, I continued to make the monthly trip with my Grandma Pearl. As she advanced in age, she preferred that I drive once I had obtained my license, a detail my mom was unaware of. Out right refused if she had anything say so. During these trips, we would stop at Circle K to buy refreshments before continuing our journey to the prison. All my grandmom requested was a cold Pepsi and some Cajun boiled peanuts. Occasionally, she would also ask for a bag of barbecue-flavored pork skins and a Hershey bar with almonds. We ensured we had single dollar bills and quarters prepared for canteen purchases and photographs during the prison visit. After two hours of travel, we arrived at our destination. At check-in, both of us were subject to searches, pat-down procedures, and had our possessions scanned for prohibited items. There were more visitors than usual during this visitation. Grandma Pearl and I chatted until my dad was allowed into the visiting lounge. I was so thrilled to see him, and I could not stop smiling, as if it were our first visit.

Dad came out with open arms, and I ran to him, feeling excited. He picked me up and I hugged him tightly. Dad commented that I was getting bigger and looked like my mom, though others said I resembled him. He was especially glad his mom, Grandma Pearl, could visit again, as he was her youngest. She said she prays God bless her to live to see him come home one day. During our visit, he was excited to tell me how he found Jesus. It changed his life, and he swore to keep God number one when he gets out. I was proud of him, and low key thinking he could save my mom from Lester. I would not dare say it aloud.

He said he earned a welding certificate, hoped to open a shop, help Leroy Jr, and support Dayshawn after his release. When I asked if he could love my mom again, Dad replied he never stopped loving her, though they could not be together—Mom struggled with addiction, and Dad always said the streets talk. We enjoyed our visit until the guards signaled it was time for the last photo. After saying goodbye, I left with four pictures of Dad for my wall. I wanted to get Grandma Pearl home before dark since she was aging, and these trips would soon be mine alone. Dad hopes for an early release and worries that losing Grandma while in prison would devastate him, as she is facing health struggles.

After pushing past the older boys to reach my apartment, I just wanted to rest. I always told mom that dad said hello, even though he had not. As soon as I entered, mom was yelling at Leroy Jr for being missing three days. Lester and his friends were partying and cutting dope on the kitchen table. The music was extremely loud, and unfamiliar guests crowded the space. Women danced with red cups while men watched. Upstairs, the smell of seafood, fried wings, and marijuana drifted into my bedroom. I opened a window, hung up my pictures, grabbed pajamas, and went for my usual shower. But this day my mom's boyfriend Lester decided he wanted to use the upstairs bathroom. I was just finishing my shower, and he entered the bathroom with force. He nearly pushed me back into the bathtub as he entered abruptly. Clearly startled by his manner, I asked him to leave the bathroom and return downstairs. Instead, he seized me by the neck and said in a slurred voice, "I pay the bills in this house, and I will use whichever bathroom I choose." The scent of alcohol and marijuana was clear on his breath. I pleaded with him to release me and tried to call out for my mom. It never crossed my mind she could not hear me from the loud blasting music and more than likely she was high on drugs or drunk. Dayshawn was in his room playing video games and usually became a zombie in trance when playing Fortnite. Lester pushed his body against mine while snatching off my towel. He gazed at my body with the evilest heinous look in his eyes. I have an unbelievably beautiful mocha complexion, took my dad's genes with my dark long curly hair but my body was all my mom. The small waist, nice small butt and thick thighs stuck to me like glue. The glimpse of Lester face sent chills down my spine, and I began to shake. I was breathing fast with fear; my eyes began to swell with tears as I continued to beg him to get out. Lester pushed me against the wall with one hand around my throat squeezing my airway, while kissing me and moving down to my breast. I tried to scream again but the sound would not come out of my mouth. All I wanted at this moment was for him to let me go or my dad burst in the door and whoop his ass. The smell of alcohol and marijuana in his breath sickened me as he continued to kiss over my body. He continued to hold his hand around my throat as he examined my body. The sound of him unzipping his pants echoed louder than you could imagine. I tried to pull up my towel and get away. He snatched my towel to the floor and push me to my knees to suck his dick. I could only imagine this being my mom's job but today her nasty boyfriend wanted her daughter to do it.

He told me what to do and dared me not to tell my mom, or he would kill me, and my brothers. He lifts me up against the wall again, thrusting with every inch of force he could inside of me. As I feel my body growing numb, all I could remember is Grandma Pearl saying to always call of Jesus in your time of need. What seemed like a lifetime was only about 10 minutes after Dayshawn knocked on the door to use it. Lester stops killing my insides and drops me to the floor. I lay there confused, crying and bleeding, as with any little girl, all I wanted was my dad.

Years went by, and I continue to endure this nightmare.

Chapter 3

My senior year of high school was moving amazingly fast. I wrote my dad several letters about Lester raping me and continued to do it repeatedly. At some point I knew my mom knew of the torture I was enduring, then again parts of me believed she did not care because he was satisfying her cravings. He would snort cocaine with my mom, have sex with her, and later come over to my room to tear up my insides. It became such a regular, that I grew numb to him, taking advantage of me. Most nights I begged Dayshawn to sleep with me just to keep

Lester out of my room. Dayshawn began to think something was happening because he had once seen Lester leaving my room and I was crying afterwards. I lied and said he was talking crap about my dad.

I tried to tell my mom on several occasions, but she was so in love with him, she accused me of wanting her man. Lester kept her high on drugs and alcohol, so she had no idea what occurred in our home. My dad would pray with me over the phone and tell me ways to defend myself. I told him about the plans I had, and my dire desire to stab Lester in the heart or poison his beer. I hope one day he will just disappear and never return to our home. Dad would encourage me to continue to pray, stay calm, clear my mind of negative thoughts, and keep DayShawn in my room at night. I really did not want to kill him; I just wanted the abuse to stop by any means. I heard my dad put a hit out on Lester for abusing me. I overheard my uncle Kevin (we call him K-boy) talking with Grandma Pearl about it.

By the second semester of my senior year, I found out I was pregnant with my mom's boyfriend baby. Sitting alone, confused, and scared, I did not know how to manage this as a young girl. I knew I could not keep this monster's baby. I wanted to talk with my mom, but I knew she would blame me for the situation. I could not dare tell my dad, I was pregnant, and I honestly believe this information would kill Grandma Pearl. I finally gained enough courage to show Lester a positive pregnancy test. He looked at me with disgust, turned around, and walked out of my room. Lester gave me money for an abortion and drove me to the women health center for the procedure. I was 18 years old therefore I did not need a parent to go with me. This sick bastard even blamed me for getting pregnant. He said I should be more responsible and take birth control. *It never occurred you have been raping me since I was sixteen!* The last two years of my life had been a living hell. I sat in the passenger seat, bleeding, cramping, crying and confused the entire ride back home.

I could not wait until I graduated and headed to the University of Southern California on an academic scholarship for Architectural and building sciences. I did not want to leave Dayshawn behind, but I was determined to get a job and have my little brother live with me. Leroy Jr was in and out of jail for selling drugs and robbing. I was so scared he would end up killed in the streets. A week before graduation, my mom found out she had liver cancer.

Grandma Pearl was in the hospital with congested heart failure, my dad had one more year before he was eligible for parole, Leroy Jr was also on the run for robbing a known mobster. I was trying to be strong for everyone including myself. My world was falling apart. I had no one to talk to. I had no clue how to repair it, so I learned how to suppress it. I learned how to smile during my pain, stay busy forgetting my past and obtain several hobbies to occupy my time. My high school years were spent as a loner. I love being by myself. It was a way to keep people out of my business and hide the secrets of my life. This was supposed to be one of the happiest moments of my life, and I am sitting here with a heavy heart, mental confusion, and broken. Everyone I wanted to share this moment with was battling a situation of their own.

I did not have any friends. I always had to fight with other girls because they did not like me for either thinking I am conceited for being cute or my good texture of my hair. I wore the latest fashion because my mom and her friends would steal our clothes or buy them from crackheads. Lester made sure to give me hush money, but he called it lunch money. I did not have any boyfriends, and Lester was sure to threaten any boy that he thought liked me in any romantic way. My dad knew of the things Lester was doing to me, but he had no idea I was pregnant and had an abortion.

I tried to seek help in high school; however, I stopped attending for a while due to the pain I would have to face and the fight with the demons from my pass. The pressure of life was growing heavy. This could not be the life of a young woman. This was not the life I imagined. I just began to fall into the Monotony of my world. No one knew of the mental and sexual abuse I endured growing up. I keep all the emotions inside of me and never talk to anyone about it. The streets took my parents away from me. I grew up distant and alone. The streets stole life from my brother, but I was determined to make it for myself, dad, Dayshawn, and Grandma Pearl.

During my first year of college, my mom passed away after her liver cancer metastasized her lungs and bones, resulting in respiratory failure. I found the situation difficult to process. I also had concerns about what would happen to Dayshawn, who was entering high school as the starting point guard on the varsity basketball team. Following my mom's death, Grandma Pearl became his legal guardian, even though she is not his biological grandmom. At that time, Leroy Jr was incarcerated, and I later learned that Lester was almost killed while in prison.

I was pleased to hear the rumor circulating about him, confident that he would eventually receive what was due to him. I secured off-campus housing to help Grandma Pearl in caring for Dayshawn. During my studies, I began employment at In-N-Out Burger. Additionally, I provided financial support to my father as he prepared his motion for the appeal board. As Grandma Pearl's health declined, I promised to graduate with honors for her. I also helped pay for Dayshawn's school needs to ease her burden. Meanwhile, I hoped my dad would receive advance release from

California before she passed away. I was trying my best to hold a 4.0 GPA. I needed to keep my scholarship and secure more money for myself. My world was dark. My heart was heavy. The walls were closing in on me. I cried every night hoping for the pain to subside. The chest pressure would let up, and the light would brighten up just enough so I could see a little clearer. I suffered with horrible depression, anxiety and even attempted suicide once. My roommate stopped me from taking a bottle of aspirin. No one knew I was dealing with several internal demons.

When I left Wilmington Arms housing projects, I left for life!

Chapter 4

My dad was granted conditional release just in time to see me graduate college. He became a father figure to Dayshawn, supporting his basketball ambitions. After two years out of prison, Grandma Pearl passed away. Several colleges recruited Dayshawn, while Leroy Jr. and my dad rebuilt their relationship and launched a successful welding business together. My dad married Charmaine, and they had a daughter, Brianna, giving me the sister I had always hoped for at age 26. As life seemed to improve, I continued working to overcome or hide past trauma.

After completing graduate school, I moved to Scottsdale, Arizona. I keep regular communication with my father, his wife, and my brothers. I have a close relationship with my younger sister, who often cares for her on weekends. Dayshawn chose to attend the University of Southern California, where he pursued basketball, and I was proud of his accomplishments. My father began attending church regularly and was later ordained as a pastor. Leroy Jr. also became a consistent attendee and met his girlfriend, Kamila, whose sincerity, and straightforward nature I appreciate. She did not accept frivolous behavior. She encouraged him to pursue a GED and welding certification, following their father's example. Life began to improve, though at times it seemed incomplete. There is hope that their mom could see the progress her children have made, and an acknowledgment of Grandma Pearl's persistent prayers.

I joined Silver Tree Architecture Concepts as an intern after completing graduate school. The position was temporary, with the possibility of securing a permanent role with the company or another firm. My goal was to seek professional opportunities regardless of my background. At Silver Tree, my personal history was not known. I chose to use the name Ashley during this time. After completing two months as an intern, I accepted a full-time project manager position and began earning a six-figure salary. I approached my career with enthusiasm and commitment. For the first time, I experienced a sense of recognition and appreciation in my professional life. During this period, I also bought my first home. However, my relationship with my father became more distant, and I had fewer opportunities to visit or spend time with my younger sister. My brother Dayshawn was playing basketball in Germany, Leroy Jr was on his third kid, and I was still waiting to get in a committed relationship. I was busy making money and gaining a name for myself. I did not have time for men, kids, church, or family. The more money I made, the more it felt good. I was finally able to suppress my pass and embrace my new future.

I reinvented myself as Ashley, distancing myself from my past in Wilmington Arms to become a wealthy social influencer admired by colleagues. I bought a $1.2 million home in McDowell Sonoran Preserve and now focus solely on making money and keeping my coworkers' respect, often concealing the truth about my background.

But to look back in retrospect on how everything started for me......

Chapter 5

One day, my executive manager entered my office. "Hello, Ashley." "Hello, Mark. How are you?" "The company is performing well, but we require you to lead a project against a strong competitor." "Of course, Mark, I am ready to take on the challenge. Who are we competing with?" "Elite Index is vying for the contract to develop the new Arizona Cardinals Stadium and the adjoining hotel." "Securing that deal would be quite an achievement." "I appreciate your positive outlook, Ashley, which is why I am assigning you to oversee this $50-

million contract." "That is a substantial amount, Mark. Are you certain?" "Yes." "Who is the primary contact at Elite Index for this competition?" "Their representative is a newcomer, Shelby Warren. Sylvester and Associates will be our contractors. Please set up a meeting with them soon to present our designs, layouts, and pricing—I want our offer given first. This deal could bring at least $500k to my team and $175k to me. I scheduled a team meeting, and everyone began working on layouts and printing ideas. *Please provide all potential designs by Friday.* I have scheduled an appointment with Sylvester and Associates.

Good morning, Sylvester, and Associates. This is Ashley Montgomery. May I speak with Mr. Sylvester Carter? He is a contractor on my project. Ms. Montgomery from the contracting company assigned Shelbie Warren as the project contact. I asked them to leave a message for both individuals, provided my contact details, and visited the company's website to find information about Shelbie Warren. As Ms. Warren was recently appointed to the company, a photograph was not yet available. More research involved reviewing earlier bidding activities associated with Sylvester and Associates and consulting colleagues within the corporate sector about Shelbie Warren's professional background. It was said that she had recently moved from Michigan to Arizona, and this little detail of information was enough to let me know that Shelbie did not know much about our area.

With little progress on Shelbie, I reached out to Sylvester and Associate before the project bid. Sylvester Carter was available and agreed to lunch at a local bistro.

I was totally shocked to see an Asian man walking in to greet me. I was looking for a clean-cut Black man especially with the name Sylvester. *Hi, I am Sylvester! Are you Ashley Montgomery*? Aww, yes! Yes, I am Ashley, genuinely nice to meet you, Mr. Carter. *Oh no, just call me Sylvester.* Please have a seat. We sat and ordered lunch. Sylvester leans in and says "I *know you just did not want to have lunch with a stranger.* Absolutely not! I want to discuss the options for my company to head up the bidding for Cardinal Stadium. I heard about Elite Index and a newcomer Shelbie Warren assigned to the project. He jokingly replied with *"is this a bribery lunch."* We shared a laugh, and I graciously replied; of course not, but deep inside it was and hopefully the beginning of something else. This man is charming and incredibly attractive. It took God time and patience when he created Sylvester. I know I did not have time for love in the middle of making money, but this one makes an exception. We shared small talk over lunch. After three hours of lunch, drinks, and meaningful conversation, we agreed to share personal contact information.

Sylvester leaned back in his chair, with his eye glazing at me with lust. He said, "I have another appointment today; however, I am interested in continuing this conversation and would appreciate the opportunity to gain experience and learn more about you. "Let's keep in touch and plan a dinner meeting to talk more about the project." He paused, then replied seriously, "I'd like that."

I permitted myself a brief return to routine amidst my responsibilities of sinking the deal. I am prepared for both giving and receiving support, and I remain optimistic about the significant opportunity facing my company.

However, I understand the importance of focusing on one priority at a time. So therefore, I would like to conquer this deal and steal Sylvesters heart afterwards.

I updated my senior partners about my perceived advantage, without mentioning my feelings for Sylvester or our planned dinner.

Two weeks have passed since Sylvester, and I had lunch. We still talk on the phone and hope to arrange dinner when our schedules allow.

It was approaching crunch time for decisions to figure out who would help head up the project. I was losing my edge with Sylvester, despite us continuing to get to know each other.

I sat in my office, with a few members of my printing team. Moments later, all the senior partners enter with celebratory champagne and clear flute glasses. Yes! Yes! Yes! My firm landed the deal. I could not be happier about the brand-new news. It was an exciting opportunity for my team in addition to lots of work with the scale of designs that will be needed for completion. I continue to celebrate with my colleagues, but I was sure to send Sylvester a text "Thank you for the deal. Dinner tonight at Dun Migos Italian Restaurant at 7p". I received a thumbs up emoji as his reply.

I did not know if I was happy because of the deal with Sylvester company or the fact we were having dinner tonight. I rushed home to get dolled up and myself together. I called my stylist, offer her $300 extra dollars to fit me in for a quick style and face beat. I wore a tight navy-blue pantsuit to bring just enough attention to the greater assets of my body. This is the first time

Ashley Montgomery thought that love would find her.

Chapter 6

The air was thick with the scent of Jasmine and the sea breeze. It had been three years since Sylvester and I met, and now the Thai coastline wedding was the backdrop. The cost was worth it. I flew with my entire family across the world to see this. The only face missing was those I cherish the most, Mom and Grandma Pearl. I could only hope they were watching. As for my dad, his composure had completely failed. His tears flowed like a river, his entire frame shaking as he performed. The singular disbelieving act of walking his only daughter down the aisle to be married.

The beautiful lives of vessels not built feel incomplete. We've been trying to have a baby for over a year now. Each month was a cycle of hope, effort, and agonizing disappointment despite our meticulous tracking, timing, and relentless efforts every attempt to conceive. Had ended in failure. Our dream of being a family began the day we were married. We have been trying to conceive tirelessly, and the reality has been. Unsuccessful. To the Council. Every careful attempt, every whispered prayer had been unsuccessful. The silence in my home where a baby's cry should be. It was becoming deafening.

We never imagined it would be this difficult to conceive. After all the failed attempts, we turned to IVF clinic, but the ongoing frustration led to tension and less intimacy between us.

Several more months have gone by. Here we are three years later without the sounds of little feet running around the house. As our focus shifted more towards work, our relationship became strained. Eventually, I asked Sylvester to try IVF again; he agreed, though he was uncomfortable with aspects of the process.

After a week of analysis, we learned that Sylvester was 100% good to conceive. Now, here I am mentally torn knowing that I have been the issue with us not getting pregnant. I agree with the recommendations to visit a specialist to help with the procedure.

Our ride home was in dead silence and later there was a horrible argument. I heard the frustration and anger in Sylvesters tone with every word he spoke.

"*Sylvester, baby I didn't know I couldn't have a baby, please believe me,*" I said between the tears that being to stream down my face. I manage to mumble words of apologetic explanation between the sobbing and gasping for a breath. Sylvester did not look in my direction. His eyes were affixed to the road, and I knew his thoughts were in the clouds. My words grew distant as the echo of my sniffles became obsolete to him, turning up the volume of the radio.

As I sat on the bed, I could not help but remember the horrible experience I had during the abortion when I was 18 years old. My virginity was robbed of me forcefully, but I was not hoping that was the direct cause. It has been 9 more months of fertility injections, appointments, blood testing, and tissue sampling. Sylvester's frustration became increasingly clear. It was clear that he harbored negative feelings towards me, often displaying expressions of disdain. He started to routinely stay away after work, which was uncharacteristic of his usual behavior. Despite my efforts to preserve our marriage, I found it difficult to understand that the issue of having a child could potentially lead to its dissolution.

As time progressed, months turned into years, and after 5 years, we are still engaged in efforts to conceive a child. Recently, Sylvester informed me about a physician in Florida who specializes in helping couples with fertility challenges. His initiative was unexpected, given our recent lack of discussion about expanding our family. Over the past year, Sylvester and I have become increasingly distant; his presence at home has diminished significantly, and I have harbored concerns about his commitment to our marriage, though I have no definitive evidence.

Nonetheless, I agreed to visit the specialist in Florida. While I have always wished to travel there, my intentions were different from our current purpose. My earlier vision involved enjoying Miami's streets in a convertible alongside my husband. Instead, we now find ourselves awaiting a consultation with Dr. Angel Ferdinand at his Boca Raton office.

"Ashley Montgomery," someone called out, but I did not see who it was. Sylvester and I headed toward the reception desk, but before we reached the nurse, a girl from Wilmington Arms started calling out "Leroya." I signaled for her to stop using my name. Sylvester, puzzled, asked if I knew her. I responded that she did not look familiar. He then asked about "Leroya," and I told him I was just being polite by waving. My real name is Leroya Ashley Montgomery, who was unknown to Sylvester, as I had changed it after leaving Wilmington Arms. It was unexpected to meet someone from California there. It was destined for me not to be here. Maybe it is a sign or something. I continue to see the mysterious look on Sylvester's faces. He

kept that incident in the back of his
mind.

Moments later we were in the office
with Doctor Fernando. The atmosphere
was sterile and quiet as he spread out the
blood tests and ultrasound reports. He
went straight into the results. My blood
levels were good, and my ovaries were
healthy, releasing viable eggs. All perfect
for conception. Then his tone shifted. I
need to ask about any history of vaginal
trauma, he said. He pointed out the
printout showing several areas of scar
tissues in my vaginal canal. The scar
tissue, he explained, was a physical

barrier, possibly preventing the sperm from reaching the eggs to fertilize them. It was not my health! That was the problem. But an internal injury, the relief of being fundamentally healthy, crashed against a sudden, shocking reality of this new obstacle. Sylvester stiffened. Besides me, Doctor Fernand explained that the ultrasound showed several areas of damage. The severity of the scar tissue in my vaginal canal he spoke about it clinically explaining how this issue could physically be blocking the sperm cells from reaching their waiting egg. But I kept thinking "my body was healthy" and

I could not understand this internally damage trauma is the reason. I suddenly felt huge and terrifying turmoil Resonated me to the core.

All I remember is the pain from Lester ripping my insides out repeatedly for 2 years. Now here I am dealing with the consequences of my innocence taken from me. And the abortion I was forced to have.

I grabbed my purse, ran out of the office balling in tears.

Sylvester was running in the far distance calling out to me.... *Ashley! What is wrong with you? The doctor is only asking questions to give us answers.* I can tell by the harsh tone of his voice and the mannerism of his posture, he was over me, this journey, and this marriage.

Sylvester demanded answers! He deserves answers but I was not ready to give it to him. My perfect life was crumbling.

We return to Arizona, in silence. Walking around our million-dollar home felt like I was living in a shopping mall alone. Sylvester slowly moved several of his items out of the house. At this point, I knew my marriage was over. He was a good man. I could not have asked for a better husband to come and love me despite my past. I kind of felt he was married to a fake version of myself. I concealed my childhood from him on purpose. He has always been a great husband. The only thing he ever asked of me was to make him a dad and I selfishly could not be honest enough to tell him the truth about the horrible events that I suppressed. Night after night, I cried, fighting the demons from my childhood. Every monster that hunted me at 15, 16 and 17 years old returned; riding my back, visiting me in my dreams, and crowding my thoughts in my mind.

I am screaming in internal agony. I am walking around in turmoil, and I am torturing myself for not being honest to the only man that has genuinely loved me besides my dad. I do not know how I can make this right and save my marriage.

Chapter 7

It has been six months since Sylvester, and I left Florida. I went to California to visit my baby sister Brianna. My dad knew something was troubling me. He at once dove in, "What *wrong baby girl*"? He leans in to kiss me on the forehead. I looked into his eyes, and tears began to roll down my cheeks. Daddy had no idea that Sylvester did not know about my true past. We hardly ever visited my family in California. Sylvester only met my dad at the wedding and once again for Christmas. I tried so desperately to hide that part of my life but now it is haunting me. "Nothing *is wrong dad, Sylvester and*

I had a little fight, I managed to utter under my sniffing. ANOTHER LIE... Lying is becoming a regular part of my life lately.

We had dinner together, watched a family movie, and I was sure to spend some time with my baby sister before I headed back to Arizona. I was hoping to see Leroy Jr and his family. But they were away on vacation in Las Vegas. I fixed a to-go plate before getting on this lonely road back home. We said our goodbyes, and I left. My dad knew something was bothering me. He did not want to be pushy; I am sure of it. Every car I passed looked like Sylvester. Every man I saw at a gas station resemble my husband. I was longing to hear his voice. We have not spoken in over four months. Sylvester has ignored all my calls, blocked my emails, and selfishly banned me from his job. All I have right now is my career to hold on to.

During my time in California, Sylvester entered our home to remove more of his belongings. I heard he had a one-bedroom condominium on the east side. I was trying to give him his space, but I wanted to work on our marriage. I wanted my husband back. I was ready to tell him everything. I was not sure how he would process the information, but I wanted to at least try. I needed to try. I tried to call his parents, but they were not too eager to hear from me. He must have mentioned we were separated or possibly facing a divorce.

I walked into the kitchen, and there it was! The day I dread. At that moment I was hoping I would never experience this. The pain that pierced my heart. The tears that swelled my eyes. The elephant that stepped on my chest to hinder my breathing and slowing increased my respirations. A white envelope with

Gardner and Associates on it. Sylvester has left me divorce papers. My friend Abby could have sent me a text message at a better time.

-*Hey girl, I am here at the Ob Gyn office, and I see Sylvester with a pregnant lady. Is everything ok with you all? Call me!*

Please Lord, please!!! Wake me from this nightmare! I know Sylvester is not divorcing me because he has moved on with another family. This is so unreal. He has only been out of the home for 6 months. He must have been seeing this woman when he left the first time. How can he do this to me? What did I do to deserve this type of pain? I closed my eyes, and when I woke up, I was lying on the cold kitchen floor. No memory of how long I was there or what happened to me. I am sure I passed out. I just remembered continually reading Abby's text message- my world went drastically dark. Again.

I needed to find out if this information was true. I logged into google to find out as much as I could and if this information were true. I spontaneously hired a private investigator. I wanted addresses, credit card statements, phone call logs, pictures, and tracking.

Two weeks later, the private investigator gave me more information than I could have asked for. He gave me Sylvester's new address, his call log and the pain that hurts the most. This man was having a baby with Shelbie Warren. The same skank I whooped in getting the business deal with Sylvesters company. How dare him slap me in the face with this woman. Out of all the women in Arizonia, he picks her! This is so intentional pain. This vindictive hurt. And she is having his baby. The never of him to move on so fast. I never knew having a baby would mean this much to him.

I cannot stop crying. I have no one to talk to. My mom and grandma Pearl passed on. I grew up alone; forced to deal with the weight of the world by myself. I did not make friends well growing up. I sheltered myself; I didn't want others to know the life I was enduring at home. I closed off my emotions to peers, teachers, and counselors that may have seen a little glimpsed of what was occurring. I cannot talk with my dad about this. He would never understand. All I have is Abby. She does not know about my past either. Here I am, sitting on the edge of my bed, hold pictures of my husband hugged up with another pregnant woman. He is happy. The kind of happiness I have never received from Sylvester. She is holding the one thing that my husband asked me for. She is carrying his life. She is carrying his heart. The more I thought about it, the more it hurt. The pain was becoming too unbearable. Too unbearable to think about and too unbearable to imagine my husbands in love with another woman.

We share lots of memories but to think about it-I cannot recall seeing my husband with this type of joy on his face. I have failed as a wife. The one thing my husband wanted from me; I could not give it to him. It was not my fault he conceived a kid during our marriage, but it was all my fault. My choice is to lie to him, and myself.

I wanted to call him so badly. I felt as if we were talking about this, things would be better. I called his office several times in the past. His secretary would say he was in a meeting or out of office. I refused to feel any added pain or embarrassment from this situation. I will just lay her holding the pictures, sleeping in agony, and accepting the misery of my actions. If

I am asleep, I will not have to deal with the reality of this.

I grabbed a bottle of Tylenol PM, popped three tablets, and chased it with a bottle of wine. I had nothing else to live for. My normalcy was no more. Maybe when I fall asleep, all this will be over in the morning.

Chapter 8

It has been 2 years since Sylvester, and I divorced. He allowed me to keep our home, since he eventually moved to Detroit with Shelbie. He sold his company to a local businessperson that's known only to flip businesses. I heard the business sold for 3.7 million dollars. He was off living his new happy life. New wife. New baby. New family. While I am here, sinking deep in depression. The unyielding of this monotony was soul snatching. I have not left my home in 2 years. I order Instacart, Uber eats and any home delivery service I can find. I quit my job, and I have been living off my saving ever since. My days are dark, gloomy, and full of pain. My best friend is a bottle of Benadryl, Tylenol PM or anything that would help me sleep my pain away. My garbage is overflowing with wine bottles, beer cans and take out boxes. I often go for days without a shower, combing my hair or even brushing my teeth. Sleep felt good! It was the only time of the day I was not faced with my dreadful life. I cut off my cell phone from the world -ignored anyone that may even mention Sylvesters name. Some days, I refused to live. I was praying for death to visit me, just so the pain would stop hurting. I tried to end it all, but God was not ready to grant my wish. The Unyielding Monotony was seriously getting the best of me. I lost my days, confused my weeks and the months felt like a lifetime. Life kept repeating itself. Repeatedly, it was eaten at my core. The vomiting and diarrhea were every day. Day after day, my world was too dark to even imagine light could ever visit me again. It had gotten so bad I forgot what living felt like. The birds stopped chirping, ducks no longer quacked, the ponds dried up, and my green grass turned brown. I pushed away family and avoided any type of interaction with human life as possible.

My dad completed a wellness check on me one day. The police asked me did I have anything to live for- "My life was stolen from me, I have nothing else, and no one to love me" They must have seen all the trash overflowing over the house and my horrible smell; I was baker act as being suicidal. I put up a fight, prohibiting them from taking me from my home. I was handcuffed, taken to jail for resist arrest because I sucker punched the officer. I spent a week in jail before I my release to **Amazing Recovery Rehabilitation Center.** Dad recommended my release to the treatment facility. My family has never seen me in this condition. He had no idea how I got to this point. I remember my dad standing there with tears in his eye, holding back every bit of emotion as he watched his baby girl walk away handcuffed and labeled a criminal. Leroy Jr and Dayshawn yelled for me to keep my head up and things would get better. Their voices seemed distant. My world was dark. Everything appeared gray. I tried to fight my way out of this depression but the more I tried to fight the sand filled around me and before I knew it, I was being pulled into a sink hole of quicksand, cement, and heavy bricks. I could not escape.

There was no way Leroya Montgomery, from Wilmington Arms housing projects, was sitting here in a mental health facility. I spent the first month confined to my room, refusing to talk to therapists, eat the food, or even take part in any group projects. What was I doing here in a facility with crazy people? These folks have serious mental issues! And this is not me. I am fine. I need to get out of here before their craziness rubs off on me. I need to go home and just be alone.

Then one day this girl named Cheryl was transferred to my room. She would read the bible all day. She spent many nights talking to me but all I could do was listen to her talk about forgiveness and how Jesus was coming to get her out of here. I continued to avoid any human interactions with anyone in the facility. Especially Cheryl. She was literally getting on my nerves talking about Jesus, forgiveness, and repentance. As each day passes. I came to realize that the only reason I am here is because of the selfishness of Sylvester and his willingness not to work on our marriage and choose another woman to be the mother of his child. This was all Sylvester's plot! How could he inflict so much pain upon me and color my world black? The more Cheryl spoke about forgiveness and redemption the more I grew angry and was full of rage and I saw nothing but red blood!

I was not trying to hear how to heal. I was too dark, wanted revenge, and was filled with enormous amounts of rage. I could taste blood. I felt the anger in the pits of my soul. The more I thought about how my life crumbled, the more I wanted to demolish everyone that took part in ripping me apart.

I have not eaten in the 6 weeks I have been here. and had no more than a sip of water when I felt thirsty. I began to hallucinate, hear voices and often had dark angels visit me with information and direction on how to deal with Sylvester, Shelbie, and anyone else from my past. Men dressed in black tackle gear would come in my room every night equip with swords and daggers. Some occasions they would try to attack me, others night they would just stand watching over me. I was eventually transferred to the local hospital for medical treatment. I was severely emaciated; the hallucinations had gotten worse. I weighed only 125 lbs. I had to be fed by IV lines and tubes placed in my stomach because I continued to refuse to eat any food.

During my admission, I met a genuinely nice nurse, Karla. She encouraged me to enjoy the meals the best I could and fight for life. She spent countless hours sitting at my bedside, talking to me, reading to me, and speaking life into me. I eventually gained strength to give a meaningful reply. The pain gradually became tolerable, the dark appeared a lighter shade of gray, but the rage stayed. My health improved enough for discharge to return to the rehab center for therapy. I just wanted to go home. I needed my bed, my body craved seclusion and doom. I knew things one day would get better, just not today. The bullet that pierced my soul was healing. The wound was still open and leaking poison. Every time I tried to bandage the site, something reminded me of Sylvester and not being able to have a baby.

I knew I was not going to get out of here until I appeared ready. I began socializing with Cheryl briefly, joined in group sessions and engrossed myself with therapy. I pretended to seem normal again. I need to fool everyone watching that I was rehabilitated enough to go home. I was ready to get out to unleash rage on Sylvester and every person that hurt me in my life. I saw red! I needed blood! I was longing to feel peace by any means necessary.

Chapter 9

These past six months in rehab were the hardest I have ever faced in my life. I finally received my walking papers to leave the facility. Life as a prisoner was hard; being released from Pelican Bay is life changing. Well at least that is what it felt like. While incarcerated in the mental facility, I had numerous visits from the dark soldiers, always standing at the foot of my bed. Vertically challenged almost eight feet tall with long dagger fingernails and dripping wet hair. The smell of septic water dripped from their pores. Garlic Vieux Boulogne cheese scent lingered in the air around them. They never mumble a word, only the look of anguish in their eyes. One night, after my usual medication, I had sunk into a deep slumber only to be visited by the dark soldiers again. They unleashed a dark plan on how to retrieve revenge on Sylvester, Shelby and Lester. The plan was meticulously methodical, I could not have come up with it myself, and I anxiously refused to wait until I came back home to put my actions into motion.

I was home. In my house. In my domicile. The only place that brought me peace. I was somewhat happy. I instantaneously grabbed my laptop to do a little research. Good ole google gave me Sylvester and Shelbie addresses in Detroit. I created fake profiles on tick Tok, Facebook and Instagram to follow them both on social media. I wanted to learn as much as I could about them both. This was definitely not the Sylvester I was married to too. This was a different man. I could barely recognize him with all the fake cheesy pictures posted on their sites. This was absolutely pathetic. The kind of pathetic that will send me to the local hospital with an elevated troponin level.

I caught a quick flight out to Detroit. I was anxious to find out as much as I could about their daily routines. I stalked them evenly for two weeks. I thought about a quick kidnap of their daughter but instead I pretended to want a job at her preschool, just to get a glimpse of her. She was ugly just like her mom. I felt sorry for a little girl walking around looking like a guppy fish shaped like Fiona from Shrek. Nothing about this little girl said Sylvester. I secretly took a picture of her even though she was such an eye sore. I snooped through the signed-out book, just to learn that

Sylvester picks her up most days. But the thing that threw me into a spiral of emotions, they named her Sylvie! That is the name Sylvester, and I talked about naming our daughter! What a bastard! He must pay! I guarantee it. After a meaningful two months away from Arizona, while briefly living in Detroit, I gained enough entailment to unleash gory sinister plot against them all.

I returned to Arizona with a full plan of rage in mind. I was ready to end it all for the pain I had felt. Homicidal ideations!

I had a list of people I wanted to make feel the same pain I felt. I was determined to find Sylvester for moving on, kill Shelbie was stealing my husband and Lester for taking any chance of me having a baby. The only time I was ever pregnant in my life was from a monster that took my innocence. I created a diabolical plant to get revenge by any means necessary. But first I had to start with the small job.

Lester is old now. I had not seen him in years. The name itself felt like grit on my tongue. Now the old bastard was tucked away at Ewell Assistant Living Facility, waiting on his final miserable days. I was not wishing him dead-not yet at least. That would be too easy. It is amazing what money can make happen, what doors it can unlock. A discreet transaction with a vocational school. A cheap laminated nurse assistant certificate slipped into a new wallet. A crisp application, perfectly innocent, submitted to the very place where the gargoyles slept. I got the job of course! Every sterile linen light. Hallway now felt like a countdown. Every shift I pulled, every resident I helped was a step closer to Room 312. I was here, I was inside, and tonight I was finally going to get my revenge.

The rubber soles of my shoes squeaked too loud on the polished floor as I slowly walked towards room 312. Every flickering of the fluorescent lights was a flash bulb going off in my skull. I could feel the cheap plastic of my ID bags sweating against my collarbone. A tremor ran through my hands, not from fear, but from the coiled frantic energy of years of waiting to get my revenge. Focus. Focus, Leroya. I forced to smile at an elderly woman shifting past me. Her vacant eyes never met mine. Nobody saw the real me. Nobody saw the evil and the rage that I had hidden in my eyes. I was just a uniform, just a ghost walking towards a closed door of room 312. The air was thick and sweet with disinfectant and regret. I scanned the hall. It was gently past midnight, and the shift change was over. Quiet, too quiet. A small, perfect window of opportunity. I move past the staff lounge, keeping my shadow tight to the wall, listening to the telltale Creek or the floorboards. Or the hiss of an overhead security camera. My blood sang. This was a moment I had replayed one thousand times in the dark in my mind. This was a moment that the Dark soldiers and I had not discussed. If anyone caught me -a nurse. A cleaner, anyone? The years of planning would vanish, and I would never get my revenge on Lester. It will be a complete ruin. I reached the corner of the brass numerals of Room 312 gleamed with happiness. I had finally reached a moment when I was extremely happy but also revengeful and hurtful. I was full of rage. My focus narrowed on the corridor ahead. Lester! Ole Lester! He had always been so careful, so untouchable. Now he was frail, helpless. I reached into my pocket of my scrubs, my fingers closing around the cold, smooth weight of the syringe. And the few pills of coumadin I stole from the

nursing medical cart. It felt heavy, a

counterweight to the whole sick world.

The last door on the left- 312. I could

hear the rhythmic, shallow wheeze of his

sleeping breath. Through the cheap wood

door. It was not the sound of a monster;

it was the pathetic sound of a target. In

the long. The air. Hallway seems still the

sound of every security system, every

sleeping resident, every cheap appliance

sound even louder tonight. I was inside, I

had the uniform, the papers. The access

and the perfect opportunity to end it all

for him. As I stood there assuring myself

that this was the route that I wanted to take. I was sure that I wanted to end it all for Lester, but I had to make sure that this was the way I wanted to end it up for him. Thoughts ran through my head. Should I use the syringe, or should I just use the pills? Maybe not tonight. I wanted him to suffer. I did not want him to find the easy way out. Immediate death would be too easy. I wanted to see the pain and the agony in his eyes. I wanted him to feel every inch of misery that I endure all the years living under the roof with him. I wanted him to feel the force of pain ripped through his body like he ripped through mine. I studied his pattern, and I learned his day-to-day routine.

Limited visitors. He would hardly eat in the cafeteria with other residents. He often walked outside to relieve stress with the smoke of a single cigarette and took a drink of his normal choice of Amsterdam. I befriended the nurse on his hallway to gain her trust. I made her believe Lester was one of the nicest residents that I have ever cared for. I continued to steal Coumadin tablets every chance I could get. I would crush the pills and place them in lusters food before I served him every meal tray.

He went to the hospital several times with gastrointestinal bleeds. During his time away from the facility, I would sneak into his room and place pesticide in his snacks and cigarettes. Lester was deathly sick day after day. No one knew I was out to end this man's life like he did mine. One night I decided to work a double night shift, I secretly entered his room 312 while he was sleeping. Miss Polly was up walking the halls as her normal 12:00 midnight stroll. I barely missed her as I gingerly entered Lester's room. She must have seen me when I entered. She turned around and asked me, was everything

OK? I lied to her, saying he needed an extra pillow from his closet. She continued to follow me into his room, but I redirected her back down the hall, making sure I put emphasis on. Mr. Lester needed his privacy and his rest. I slowly approached his bed-the slow anticipation of my methodical plan grew more enticing. As I continued to approach his bed, standing there looking over his lifeless body while watching the rise and fall of his chest. Hearing the wheeze of his breath with every inhalation and exhalation grew exponentially.

I graciously placed a pillow over his head to suffocate him to death. His weak frail frame could not conjure enough strength to fight or even give a squeal of agony. Uh. This sickens me! He would not even contest the action of dying. I wanted him to suffer. I needed to punish him. He was dying too easily.

Since the coumadin caused him to have an ocular bleed which led to partial blindness, he had no idea it was me. I held the pillow over his head just enough to have him gasping for air. He would lift in a cold sweat as if he just had a nightmare. Night after night I worked in his hallway and caused him endless pain. I gave him ice cold showers, beat him with wet towels, and put itching powder in his brief. Everything in me, wanted to end his man hood. I hated the sight of it. He did not deserve to urinate from it. I taped his mouth with duct tape and stuck enema bottles up his rectum. I poured hot cups of tea on his private parts. He screamed in pain; I love the sight of agony on his face. Just seeing him squirm, roll around in bed and yell for help gave me peace and pleasure. I was able to see light now.

I whispered in his ear. *"This is Leroya from Wilmington Arms housing projects"* *Do you remember me? You ruined my life! You took everything from me!*

You killed my mom with drugs; you ruined my life as a child. You robbed me of my innocence, you nasty bastard. And you will pay!

I had decided I was ready to give myself a moment of lasting desire and excitement. I return to work with great hopes of letting this be my last night seeing Lester alive. The step I took was a sacrifice, severing the last fragile thread to a normal life. I was done with trying to forget. I was ready to claim a lasting desire and excitement. A final, brutal situation. I was walking into my last night of ever seeing Lester breathe air. The knowledge was a glorious, freezing rush through my body, with poisoned needles clenched tight in each hand, the silver sharp points cold anchors in my sweating palms. I just hoped this would be the last night of me carrying his savage beast in my spirit. I knew it! I knew it in my soul. He will be rolled out of her on a gurney.

I pushed open the door to his room. The hinge is given a soft compellent sound. I give a Sigh. A small painful gasp. In the sudden silence, the bed was stripped empty. Empty! I grit my teeth in frustration. The shot was a physical blow, still in my momentum and leaving me vibrating with a sense of adrenaline rushing through my core. My grand, terrifying intent had nothing left to strike. I spawned to the nurse's station, my voice a little strained, brittle and wired. Where is he? Where is he? She looked up, a plastic mask of tire professionalism that flattered slightly under my intensity. He... he went home with his family. She hesitated, her eyes flickering from my face to the needles, which I suddenly realized. I still held out in the open, but something inside of me felt she was not telling me the truth. She swallowed hard, lowering her voice to a defensive murmur. He was transferred earlier to the hospital for rectal bleeding.

He bled out before doctors could get him into surgery. I could not say I was not happy. This was the best news I heard all day. Fate served him his just reward after all.

Chapter 10

I continue to work at the assistant living facility for 3 more weeks. I stole needles, syringes, roll gauze and tape. I still had a little coumadin left over from giving it to Lester. After quitting that useless employment, I made another trip to Michigan. I followed Shelbie to and from her spa appointments, hair salon, and grocery shopping. She kept the same routine, time for appointments and route to pick up their daughter. I was determined to make her pay for stealing my husband from me. I wanted to taste her blood on a stick. I was longing to see the guts hanging out of her stomach, and brain matter scattered across the road. She stole my husband, and she will pay! The masterplan was still in the beginning stages. I was not sure what I really wanted to do but I just knew I needed to do something. It took lots of planning to figure out how I wanted to attack her.

One day Shelbie parked in the local mall parking garage. I knew this had to be the perfect time to implement part of my plan to destroy her. She deserved to feel all the hurt, shed tears, and suffer the agony as I felt. I parked the rental car next to her Mercedes. I was sure to back into the parking space so my tag would be hidden from on lookers. Luckly for me, Shelbie parked the opposite angle for the garage cameras and gave a perfect opportunity for me to unleash my deviance. I slipped out of the car door and crawled under her car. I had no idea what line her breaks were, so I decided to cut every wire that seemed important. Several liquids started squirting out, even hitting me in the face. Thank God it missed my eyes. I was sure to wear gloves dress in a dark hoodie with boots. More than a few episodes of Law and Order taught me a tip or two.

I quickly got back in my car when I heard some people walking in my direction. I turned in my seat, as if I were talking with someone in the back seat of my car until they were out of sight. I sped away and hit the interstate for the airport. I boarded my plane early and headed back to Arizona. A few days later I saw on Sylvesters social media, he was asking for prayers for his wife. She was in tragic car accident, and he needed help. He said she was fighting for her life in the ICU. I was so disappointed with my work! Now, I am sitting with thoughts wondering if I should enter the hospital to finish her off.

Here I am, pacing the floors of my home, trying to construct another plan to make Sylvester hurt! The fury was overcoming my thoughts. All I wanted was revenge. I could taste it. I breathe it. I felt it. I sat at my laptop and typed a nice empathetic post to Sylvester. He replied and thanked me for my nice kind words. I continued to watch him post the stages of her condition and the road to her recovery. Two months later, Shelbie came home. I sent yellow roses to their home with anonymous card that read.

"I *was saddened to hear about the details of your accident*."

Well, I did not lie this time! I was saddened that she was still alive. I sat staring out the window at the dried-up pond in my yard. I missed the calmness of the ducks swimming. But the eyesore was dreadful. I spent the next three months learning increasingly amounts of information on vengeance. Luckly for me Sylvester's dad passed away. That meant he would be returning to Arizona. I had to think quickly! I would attend the funeral services to gain more intel on Slyvester and Shelbie. I went to a local wig vendor and bought a cinnamon burgundy wig. It gave me the incognito look for which I was searching. I bought an old lady dress to resemble one of his dad's church members. I sat in the back of the church as Sylvester and Shelbie walked hand in hand. She had a little limp from the thanks of me. I signed the obituary book as "Le Webster." No one recognized me- not even Sylvester! I wanted to push him into the burial hole with his dad. But that would have been too obvious. Therefore, I settled for returning to the church to help with the repass. I personally made a nice plate for Sylvester to eat. I loaded his lemonade up with MiraLAX and melted chocolate ex-lax and poured it over his cake. If I could not get him now, I wanted him to spend his evening grieving his dad on the toilet. I needed to get Shelbie again, but she was suffering enough.

There is a part of me who really feels bad about the things I have done to Sylvester and Shelbie. There is a part of me that has a conscience but then again, the rage is too intense to deal with. The feeling of dread and morn is felt in my core as if I lost a baby for real. I did lose a child. I lost the opportunity to have the perfect family I dreamed of having. There were a lot of missing pieces that I could blame for the pain I was feeling with losing my husband. But I was not going to blame myself even though I could have told Sylvester about my past. I needed to escape that part of my reality. It sickens me to the stomach to relive the torture of Lester getting off in me. And I refused to relive those moments to recall the story to tell my husband. I was sure he would not understand since he was adopted into a wealthy loving family. I was not sure if he would have even understood the dread of indirectly protecting a pedophile. I came from the bottom of the barrel. I defeated every challenge I was faced with as a kid. Even being raped night after night by a low life drug addicted pedophile. I still wonder how he could engage in sexual relationships with my mom, then finish his sexual urges with her daughter. Here I am sitting with tears in my eyes, wishing I could talk with Grandma Pearl or even my mom. I occasionally talked to the dark soldiers that sit at the foot of my bed. I was hoping to reduce the stimulation for the desire to see red or should I say blood. The dark soldiers would always give me advice on how to get back at Sylvester and Shelbie.

Nevertheless, I made it out the pits of hell. I showed resilience, and overcame every one of the difficult, dark traumatic incidents of my childhood. One day I wish to make it out of this head space I have been living in for years.

Chapter 11

It seemed like eternity. The dread of the horror continues to hunt every part of me. The idea of Shelbie still having breath in her lungs sickened me with every thought of the idea. Closing my eyes, imagining her cuddled up in the arms of my husband Sylvester made me appreciate every visit from the dark soldiers. I felt like I had one last time to release the most diabolical plan of all. It was a demonic sinister idea that was conveyed by a deep sense of hurt and misery. This was my last chance. I needed to inflict as much pain, agony, and rage as I could on Shelbie and

Sylvester. I could taste the salt in the blood as it filled the jaws of my mouth. As the sensation dripped down the back of my throat, I could feel the warmth traveling to the guts of my soul. Finally, a moment of fresh air. This felt good. I was beginning to see some light shining into my dark existence.

I had recently learned that Sylvester and Shelbie would be travelling back to Arizona for his parents' 50th anniversary. I had to move quickly. I had to think quickly. I did not have much time to infiltrate the event. I learned the family hired Zebabies Catering Company to serve the delicacies, entrees, and drinks for the party. There were so many people in and out of the event hall. Several different companies were setting up floral arrangements, table settings, and DJ booth with a disco floor. I must say Seven Sixteen Elegant Events and Floral were doing a phenomenal job with the décor. They hardly even notice me in the kitchen putting cyanide poison in each one of the food trays. I added antifreeze to the lemonade, Rohypnol in the sweet tea, Ketamine in the potato salad, crushed magic mushrooms into the ground meat, and put angel trumpets in the desert dishes. I wanted everyone at this event to die. I want to wipe out the entire family line of Sylvester and Shelbie, especially his parents because they knew he was seeing Shelbie behind my back. I am sure they were the motivation behind his actions to divorce me. Everyone here should be dead by 6:00pm, I will just wait across the street to see the horror unfolds.

As I watched, the yard pulsed with energy; people were laughing and playing music, balloons bobbled in the air and their older family members strolled and socialized with each other.

Then suddenly a loud scream pierced the laughter. People dropped, doubled over with stomach pains, gasping for air. Their eyes wild with delirium. The sight became terrifying. Older women laying lifeless filled the yard. Men tore off their clothing and stumbled naked into the venue and many guest were violently vomiting. More screams lingered in the atmosphere. The environment swelled with frantic, confusion and turmoil.

Despite the surrounding horror, a strange joy and harmony pierce within my soul. It was then, I realized Shelbie was not amongst those collapsing in pain, and Sylvester was missing too. I ducked around the venue, keeping incognito with a pair of binoculars. I resumed my observation of the horror developing with pure happiness. The chaos was overwhelming yet deep with amusement in my core, and its miserable joy brought peace to the darker side of me. Everyone was running in circles frantically, yelling with panic.

Still no sight of Slyvester and Shelbie. Then abruptly....

There they were! Walking hand and hand like zombies, footsteps staggering, in a daze of euphoria that brought them both to their knees. Shelbie clinches her abdomen in pain. Is she dead? She is lying face down smothered in the Bahia grass on the lawn. Sylvester is crying uncontrollably, looking at his wife dying from some type of poison she ingested.

Screams! Yelling! Sight of disarray is a delight to me. I have never felt so much bliss in one setting. The bright light shining on my skin felt great.

After that brief sensation of cheerfulness, I hear a siren, loud horns and bells ringing in a distance....

Is it an ambulance? Maybe they're here to haul away all the deceased bodies lying across the soft green lawn. Or maybe the local police department to haul me off to jail again. Did someone see me on camera placing poison in the food? Was I not sneaky enough with my plan? The dark soldiers must have called and said I was guilty of this massacre.

Ashley! Ashley! Who could be calling me by name? Who even knew I was here? I cannot move. Not a limb on my body has a muscle attached to a bone for movement. The person calling my name is growing closer to me. Now I have a touch on my shoulder. I am extremely afraid to turn around to see who this could be. The light is bright shining on me. As the light brightened, I just knew the feeling of joy would be overwhelming the circumstance however it appeared dreadful.

The hand on my shoulder begins to shake me. Shake me vigorously. My vision grew dim. My eyesight was a bit blurry, but there before stood Sylvester. He leaned in to kiss me. Gingerly placing a kiss on my lips as he had done previously. Things are starting to become clear....

Why are these medical people standing over me? Where am I? What could have happened? I was just watching Shelbie die, and within a blink of an eye, I am lying in a hospital bed, hooked up to an IV line, with cords attached to my chest. How did I get here? Sylvester baby, I mumble with a scratchy throat. "What are you doing here? Where is Shelbie"?

Slyvester gives me a look of puzzlement with a grumbled reply, *"Who is Shelbie"?* She is your wife, Slyvester! The woman you left me for. The woman you had a baby with.

He sits down beside me, with a tight grip on my hand. Ashley, I have no idea what you are talking about. You have been in a coma for at least 4 weeks. I am sure you had plenty of nightmares and dreams while you were in a coma. Even at times, you were seen with strange facial gestures and moaning. You ran out of the doctor's office in Florida, stumbled over a large bolder rock, and hit your head. You have suffered a major concussion. I have been by your side since that incident occurred. Your dad, Leroy Jr, and Dayshawn have been worried sick about you. During your coma you were yelling out the name "Lester." I tried to wake you, but not anything would bring you out of the comatose state. Baby!

I am glad you are back. I was worried sick, thinking I may have lost you Ashley.

Sylvester's words really got to me. Like, where have I been for the past few weeks? The whole coma thing is a massive shock. I started crying and it hit me. I must be 100% honest with him about my life. I am pretty nervous about how he may react. Though and whether it is going to change things between us. Learning about the coma was a huge punch to the gut. I started crying even harder. It's definitely time to lay all my cards on the table with him about my life.

Chapter 12

My discharge finally came after a few more weeks in the hospital. I walked into a home where Sylvester had become my world. He was the perfect husband, the kind who does not just help but devote himself completely. He waited on me hand and foot, his love manifesting. And his ability to anticipate my needs and have everything I require ready and waiting by taking time off work he made sure my return was a seamless transition back to the life I knew.

One day Sylvester and I were sitting at the table having dinner. I mentioned the idea of us having a baby again and the things that came out during our visit to Doctor Ferdinand office in Florida.

Sylvester stared at me, clearly curious. I realized he had wanted to discuss this since my discharge but was waiting for me to bring it up. After a deep breath, I began: "Sylvester, there are things about me you've never known, and it's been unfair to keep them secret." Sylvester pushed back in his chair, placed his fork down on the hard wood and crossed his arms in a manner of defense and his undivided attention. "I don't know where to start Sylvester" He leaned up, with both elbows on the table with his hands in a prayer state.... *Just try!*

It took everything in me to utter the words....

My name is not Ashley Montgomery. I was born Leroya Ashley Montgomery. His eyes grew big! He was calm and allowed me to finish my story. I begin to cry while reliving the horror of my childhood and telling him about the name "Lester." I spent the next few hours overwhelmingly expressing the pain, trauma, toxicity, violence, rape, drugs, abuse, isolation, and resentment.

"Sylvester! Say something please" This man sat before me, with perplexity across his face. This was immense amount of information inundated at one time. He needed space to process things. I rose from the table, walked to the bedroom, and sat on the edge of the bed. I was shaking in nervousness. I was not sure if I had developed Parkinson disease or had a seizure. Snot pouring from bilateral nostrils, sea saltwater running down my face and here he comes walking in....

His fists are clinched! I can see the anger in his eyes. At that moment rage was seeping from his core. He proceeds towards the closet, grabbed a box from overhead, reached inside, and pulled out a –

He turns around and points it in my direction. There I stare at the black shiny cover of a bible given to him by his late great grandmother. He reaches out for my hand and pulled to the floor of our bedroom. There we both lie, crying uncontrollably, and clinching the bible. Simultaneously, I remembered the prayer Grandma Pearl taught me. We both recited Psalm 23.

The LORD is my shepherd, I lack nothing....

After an extensive amount of time on our knees praying, Sylvester looked into my eyes with forgiveness. I was remembering of the sincere love between a man and woman. It was a feeling I have never felt before. My husband honored me, adored me, and appreciated me. His kissed my forehead and said, *"I can only imagine the pain and fear you have been living with; I am sorry Leroya."*

He called me Leroya!

Chapter 13

Sylvester and I sat side by side on the sofa, a heavy leather-bound photo album room on my knees. He leaned in, his shoulder nearly brushing up against mine, and pointed to a faded. Picture of us on the beach. This was our first anniversary. He murmured. His voice was low and steady. I was forced to laugh, but the sound felt empty. A stranger's echoed in my throat. I stared at the girl in the photo. My hair was beautiful. Whipped in the wind with a bright smile, and I felt absolutely nothing. I was no longer this person in the photo. This person sustained pain, lies and deception.

The silence afterwards stretched thin. I could hear the soft whir of the clock on the mantlepiece and the occasional shift of the albums stiff pages as it closed. I avoided Sylvester's eyes. I knew what they had- flicker of a heart, quietly masked. After a long moment, he finally broke the quiet, his voice gentle. "Tea honey"? I can make your favorite Peppermint tea.

We decided to take a walk along the east river of the Arizona canals. This was one of our favorite past times. The air was thick and heavy, smelling of low tide and old wood from the pilings, but I could not connect with the scent of a single memory. Sylvester walked a step ahead, his shoulder set occasionally. Kicking a loose Pebble toward the waves, I studied the profile of his face, the familiar hook of his nose, the worried crease between his brows, and tried to force a flash of recognition. I kept my hand shoved deep into my pockets. Deep in the fabric, because I did not want to reach for him and have a gesture felt like a lie to us both.

He finally stopped by a cluster of seaweed slick rocks, turning to me. The setting of the sun had painted the sky a beautiful impossible orange. But all I could focus on was the careful, unexpected look in his eyes, searching for something in mind that was not there. My memory continues to show improvement. But it just was not where it should be. The walk along the water did not feel like a history lesson anymore. It was just a quiet day. The sun was low, casting that soft, forgiving light that always made the tiny wrinkles around Sylvester's eyes show. When he smiled, he was talking about something mundane, the absurdity of the bird trying to steal a French fry from a tourist, and I found myself laughing for the first time, the sound feeling organic. Like it belonged to me. It felt real, it felt original. It felt like mine.

I stopped trying to fish for memories and simply focused on the feeling and the enjoyment of being back with my husband. The filling of his palm, rough and entirely familiar, holding my hand against his thumb swept slightly across my knuckles, a movement that had to be muscle memory for him, yet it felt like a silent, easy conversation between us. When we got to the end of the pier, he did not ask if I remembered this spot. Instead, he just pulled me close to his chest, letting me lean my head against a familiar solidness of his shoulder. It was not fireworks or a grand declaration. It would. A steady low humming of warmth that said I am here we are okay regardless of what you recall. This moment felt familiar, and it allowed me to forget all the hurt and the pain that I had endured. True love was not in the past we were trying to recover, but in an effortless way we fit back together. Like two puzzle pieces that recognized their shape even after the picture on them had faded.

Here I am reflecting on the things that caused me pain in my childhood. Deep inside I was wanting to see what ever happened to Lester. I heard he died in a prison riot. I found purpose in my pain. I longed for Grandma Pearl and my mom. I was happy to still have my dad, Leroy Jr. and Dayshawn. Not to mention a new little sister Brianna. My consciousness was clear, but something was still missing.

Chapter 14

Weeks became months, then years. Now, at 27 weeks pregnant with our first child, Sylvester and I are thrilled. Despite challenges, this pregnancy has been joyful, thanks to my supportive husband. My mom and Grandma Pearl would be so proud of me. The things science said could happen, prayer made reality. I will soon be a mother to a beautiful baby girl. We plan to name her Sylvie Monika Tenshi Carter. I cannot wait to give her all the love I missed out all growing up. The moments of watching my mom being torn away from her kids by the power of drug addiction.

Thanking Grandma Pearl for what she gave even despite her not having anything to offer but love. Leroy Sr. did not run away from his responsibilities of being a dad while incarcerated. He gave mentorship, encouragement, and endless support. Despite the circumstances that surrounded my childhood, I found my way out. I was no longer subjected to the stereotype of a poor little ghetto girl from New Wilmington Arms housing projects. That stigma is no longer attached to me. I now stand as a strong educated woman who defeated all odds against her. I am a surviving daughter, a wife and soon to be mom. I am the best sister any sibling could wish for. And an amazing daughter might I add.

Chapter 15

In retrospect, the day I ran out of the doctor's office in Florida, from the harsh reality of truth, according to Sylvester, I fell and hit my head on a huge rock. My ride home in silence was the long journey to the hospital. During my time there I battled with subconsciousness of existence. Ashley and Leroya battled for placement in my life. I was living the life of one but deep inside I knew I was the other. As the days went on Sylvester needed to divorce Ashley for the reason that was hidden in his soul. He was attracted to Leroya. He fell in love with Leroya, but she was living a lie. Not just to herself but the deception she gave to others. Suppression of life's toxicity surface and began to leak poison like an infections abscess. The thoughts that surrounded Lester were the inner darkness that started to seep from the crevasses that were only secured with paper tape and rubber bands. Death became the only outlet I wanted for him. I crave it. I tasted it. I needed it. I played out the inner script of a story buried deep into my soul about Lester. It was surfacing from the roots of hatred gathered from years of abusive seeds planted throughout my childhood.

All those emotions projected hatred towards Shelbie. But she was the person I needed to develop into. She was the only person who appeared to have Sylvesters heart. He made changes for her. He left his normalcy for her. She was the fictious character I created to compete against Ashley, not realizing Leroya was the only person who Slyvester really was in love with. But Shelbie had to die for Leroya to live. This realism found its presence when the battle between life and death started to appear as dark soldiers standing at the foot of my bed. Their muteness set up logic, sentiment, and belief. Giving me the chance to decide to fight the shadows or succumb to their way of life. Who knew a tap on the shoulder would save my life just in time before I became tragedy to my circumstance.

To clarify on the lighter side of things, the alleged murder of Lester did not take place, nor did I surreptitiously attend my husband's family anniversary dinner or engage in any act of poisoning. involved in a secret relationship with my husband, and I categorically deny any involvement in actions leading to an accident by tampering with brake lines.

Furthermore, at no point was I incarcerated or admitted to a rehabilitation facility. The so-called "dark soldiers" existed solely as constructs of imagination, hallucinations, and such experiences may only be attributed to the effects of a coma.

But to look back at this life journey, it all had to happen for a reason. The direct healing I needed to face the dark inner demons that were unknowingly haunting me.

Thank you for reading.

Challenge your imagination!